Bright =Summaries.com

The Human Beast

by Émile Zola

BOOK ANALYSIS

Written by Cécile Perrel
Translated by Oliver Brown

The Human Beast

BY ÉMILE ZOLA

Bright
Summaries.com

ÉMILE ZOLA

FRENCH WRITER AND JOURNALIST

- **Born in 1840 in Paris**

- **Died in 1902 in the same city**

- **Some of his works:**

  - *Nana* (1880), novel

  - *Au Bonheur des Dames* (1883), novel

  - *Germinal* (1885), novel

Émile Zola is considered one of the most important novelists of the 19th century in France. He is best known as the leader of the naturalist movement, which sought to apply the experimental scientific methods of the time to literature: after observing reality, Zola formulated a hypothesis and verified it by experimentation in his works. The novel cycle of the *Rougon-Macquart*, the author's main work, is an illustration of this aesthetic. This fresco of twenty books was a great success despite numerous criticisms.

Zola is also famous for the positions he takes, which often lead to condemnation. The most notorious of these is the Dreyfus affair, where his pamphlet *J'accuse…!* (1898) contributed greatly to the successful outcome of the trial of Captain Dreyfus (1859-1935).

THE HUMAN BEAST

CRIMINAL CASE IN THE ROUGON-MACQUART FAMILY

- **Genre:** novel

- **Reference edition:** *La Bête humaine*, Paris, Gallimard, «Folio classique» collection, 2003, 512 p.

- **1st edition:** 1890

- **Themes:** naturalism, heredity, murderous impulses, crime, violence, personification

The seventeenth novel in the *Rougon-Macquart* series, *La Bête humaine* was first published as a serial in the newspaper *La Vie populaire* before appearing in volume in March 1890.

In this work, Zola tells the story of Jacques Lantier, a railway engineer on the Paris-Le Havre line. He is marked by a morbid heredity and murderous impulses that keep him away from women. Despite his precautions, he falls for the pretty Séverine Roubaud, wife of a colleague, and begins to have an affair with her, until his evil reappears and makes him commit the irreparable.

SUMMARY

CHAPTER I

Roubaud, deputy head of the Le Havre station at the Compagnie de l'Ouest, spends the day in Paris where he has been summoned by his management. After his appointment, he waits for his wife, Séverine, who has taken advantage of the trip to do some shopping. When Séverine arrives, the couple have a quiet lunch, but the tone rises when Roubaud learns that the ring Séverine has always worn was given to her by magistrate Grandmorin, her godfather, who raised her and abused her when she was only a child. Thinking that Séverine is Grandmorin's mistress, he beats her. Mad with jealousy, he then decides to kill Grandmorin. He sets a trap for him with the help of Séverine, who is too terrified to attempt any kind of rebellion. In a letter, she asks him to take the train from the capital to her Norman estate. Once the letter is gone, the couple goes to the station to take the same train back to their home in Le Havre.

CHAPTER II

Jacques Lantier, one of the mechanics of the Compagnie de l'Ouest, arrives at the Croix-de-Maufras, on the railway line between Paris and Le Havre. He comes to greet his aunt Phasie who took care of him when he was a child. She lives with her daughter, Flore, and her husband, Misard. Nearby is a large, unoccupied bourgeois house belonging to Grandmorin, which is to go to Séverine Roubaud in her will.

Aunt Phasie recently lost her second daughter in strange circumstances: while Louisette was a maid at Grandmorin's house, one night she fled to the house of a neighbour, Cabuche, badly injured. She died of her injuries after telling the police that Grandmorin had tried to abuse her. The story was hushed up. Jacques, driven by curiosity, breaks into Grandmorin's estate, where he finds Flore, who is infatuated with him. As she offers herself to him, Jacques flees, overcome by the evil that has always gnawed at him: when confronted with a woman, he is tormented by the desire to kill. He walks for a long time along the railway tracks. When the train from Paris passes by, he sees a man cutting the throat of another man in one of the carriages. Disturbed, he goes back to his aunt's house, but on the way he meets Misard, who tells him that he has discovered a corpse on the track. The two men approach it: it is Grandmorin. When the police arrive, Jacques wonders whether he should reveal what he has seen.

CHAPTER III

The next morning, Roubaud, nervous, takes up his post at Le Havre station. He learns from a dispatch that President Grandmorin has been found dead on the side of the track going from Paris to Le Havre. The station master, remembering that Roubaud had returned the day before by the same train, questions him. Séverine is also called in, so that she can corroborate her husband's statements. They confirm having met the president, but they did not make the trip together. In the meantime, Jacques arrives and tells them what he saw the night before.

CHAPTER IV

M. Denizet, the examining magistrate in charge of the Grandmorin case, summons the Roubaud couple, Grandmorin's daughter and her husband, Jacques Lantier and Mme Bonnehon, the victim's sister. After reading the will of the deceased, it appears to him that the bequest of the house of the Croix-de-Maufras could constitute a good motive; his suspicions are therefore focused on the Roubauds. When Jacques is questioned, he realises that Roubaud is the exact portrait of the murderer he saw on the train. But, troubled by Séverine, he keeps quiet. Finally, the judge arrests Cabuche, the Misard's neighbour who had come to Louisette's house to die and who had sworn, at the time, to avenge her. When he leaves the judge's chambers, Roubaud, who has realised that Jacques knows something, decides to follow the mechanic: he wants to keep an eye on this troublesome witness.

CHAPTER V

Séverine goes to Paris, to see Mr Camy-Lamotte, who is in charge of putting Grandmorin's papers in order; she wants to make sure that the letter she had sent him has not been found. Camy-Lamotte receives her with curiosity, as he has found the letter and suspects the young woman of being the author. Through a subterfuge, he manages to get her to write a letter and has to face the facts: it is indeed Séverine who wrote the letter. He immediately understands that the Roubaud couple is guilty, but to charge them would weaken the Compagnie de l'Ouest. He therefore prefers to keep quiet. Séverine then finds Jacques and, before going home, they go for a walk. The young woman realises that the mechanic is attracted to her. He half-heartedly admits to her that he knows the truth, but promises not to reveal anything. The idea that Séverine is a murderer gives her a special aura in his eyes.

CHAPTER VI

A month has passed since the murder of Grandmorin. The case has been closed, Cabuche has been released and the Roubauds seem to be calm. The only shadow is the watch and money they stole at the time of the murder and are hiding at home.

Jacques and Séverine develop a tender relationship and start seeing each other on the sly. With her, Jacques is happy and his desire to kill disappears. They soon become lovers and take a trip to the capital every Friday, the day Jacques drives the train. For his part, Roubaud starts gambling and getting into debt.

CHAPTER VII

The following Friday, near La Croix-de-Maufras, the train stops, blocked by snow. The clearing of the snow takes a very long time, so Misard suggests to Séverine to come and warm up at his place. It is there that Flore overhears a kiss between Jacques and the young woman. Anger rises inside her. When the train finally sets off again, the Lison (the locomotive), damaged, does not react as well.

CHAPTER VIII

As the train arrives in Paris very late in the evening, the return journey is not scheduled until the following day. Jacques and Séverine spend the night together. Séverine suddenly feels the need to confide in him and tells him about Grandmorin's murder. Jacques questions her at length about what she felt when she killed him, and his murderous impulses return.

CHAPTER IX

In Le Havre, Roubaud is increasingly absent due to his gambling, and his debts grow larger. He then starts stealing from the loot he stole from Grandmorin on the day of his murder. When Séverine realises that her husband has spent it all, she goes into a rage and takes the watch, which she entrusts to Jacques so that Roubaud cannot use it to clear his debts.

While the two lovers are in each other's arms in the Roubauds' flat, the husband appears and surprises them. As he has no reaction, Jacques and Séverine decide to stop hiding. However, Roubaud bothers them and they decide to kill him. One night, while Roubaud is on guard and making his rounds in the station, Jacques, armed with a knife, and Séverine follow him. But, at the last moment, Jacques cannot bring himself to strike.

CHAPTER X

Flore, still furious, wants to take revenge on Séverine, and it is Cabuche who unintentionally gives her the means to carry out her plan. As the Friday train is about to arrive, Cabuche arrives in front of his neighbours' house with a cart full of stones; Flore takes advantage of this to push the car onto the track. The train hits the cart head-on, creating a terrible derailment. Séverine and Jacques are unhurt, but the accident leaves 15 dead and 32 seriously injured. Desperate and aware of the horror of her action, Flore throws herself under a train. Meanwhile, Séverine moves Jacques into her house at the Croix-de-Maufras.

CHAPTER XI

Jacques is recovering from his superficial wounds. Cabuche, secretly in love with Séverine, is very present, helping the young woman with the housework. After ten days, the doctor authorises Jacques to return to work; he spends one last night with Séverine in the house of the Croix-de-Maufras. However, the young man is uneasy because his murderous impulses are getting stronger and stronger.

The lovers decide to set a trap for Roubaud. They intend to bring him into the house, kill him, and then throw the body on the road to make it look like a suicide. However, nothing goes according to plan. Going mad, Jacques grabs the knife that was meant to be used to slit Roubaud's throat and kills Séverine before fleeing. He brushes past Cabuche who was prowling in the garden, but Cabuche does not recognise him and enters the house, where he finds Séverine lying on the floor. At that moment Roubaud and Misard arrive.

CHAPTER XII

Three months have passed since Séverine's death. Cabuche has been arrested for the murder of the young woman, but also for that of Grandmorin. As for Roubaud, he is in prison for having ordered both murders. He is suspected of having had Grandmorin killed in order to receive the inheritance promised to his wife more quickly, and of having wanted to get rid of Séverine in order to enjoy the money alone. Both men are sentenced to life imprisonment.

As for Jacques, he has taken up his post on a new train. But animosity grows with his driver because Jacques is having an affair with his mistress. One evening, the driver arrives at work completely drunk and refuses to obey Jacques' orders. They come to blows while the train is being thrown onto the tracks. During the fight, they fall and are torn apart by the wheels.

CHARACTER STUDY

JACQUES LANTIER

Jacques Lantier is a tall, dark-haired young man of 26: "A handsome boy with a round, regular face, but spoiled by strong jaws. His hair, planted hard, curled, as well as his moustaches, so thick, so black, that they increased the paleness of his complexion." (p. 65). Abandoned by his parents, he was brought up by his Aunt Phasie, for whom he has a deep affection. He attended the Ecole des Arts et Métiers and, on leaving, chose to become a railway mechanic, attracted to the solitude of the job.

Since his adolescence, he has been subject to violent headaches that plunge him into a state of unconsciousness. He is often taken by violent impulses, dreaming of shedding blood and experiencing the sensations that a murderer feels when killing. He is especially troubled by the company of women, and for this reason he flees from them. The story is about his struggle not to become a monstrous man. Despite this, he has an affair with Séverine, the wife of the sub-chief of the Le Havre station, leaving behind his cousin Flore, who is in love with him. Even though he seems to be free of his impulses for a while, he ends up slitting his mistress's throat, but is not arrested.

He dies in an argument with his train driver when he falls on the track. He is a psychologically ill man. Aware of his condition, he tries to escape his neuroses, but in vain: at the end of the novel, his bestiality triumphs.

SÉVERINE ROUBAUD

Séverine Roubaud is a young woman of 25: "She seemed tall, slim and very supple, yet fat with small bones. She was not pretty at first, with a long face, a strong mouth, lit up by admirable teeth. But, looking at her, she was seductive by the charm, the strangeness of her large blue eyes, under her thick black hair." (p. 33). She arouses the desire of all the men in the novel: she is Roubaud's wife, the former "mistress" of President Grandmorin, and Jacques' lover; Cabuche is secretly in love with her and even the general secretary Camy-Lamotte speculates about blackmailing her to obtain her favours.

She is the daughter of Grandmorin's gardener. After the death of her father, she is taken in by Grandmorin, who is also her godfather. When she married Roubaud, the couple came under the protection of the magistrate. He left her the Croix-de-Maufras property in his will. We learn later that Séverine, abused by Grandmorin when she was young, is his "mistress", which drives her husband mad with jealousy when he finds out. She helps him to kill the magistrate, but from that moment on, her relationship disintegrates. She then takes Jacques Lantier as her lover, who ends up killing her.

At the beginning of the novel, she appears as a fragile and docile young woman; she obeys Grandmorin without thinking and he takes advantage of her physically, then she obeys her husband by helping him murder their protector. But gradually, she leaves her passivity to become the one who incites to evil: during her affair with Jacques, she pushes him to kill Roubaud.

ROUBAUD

Roubaud is approaching forty, has red and curly hair: "His beard, which he wore full, was also thick, of a sunny blond. And, of average height, but of extraordinary vigour, he liked his person, satisfied with his slightly flat head, with a low forehead, a thick neck, and a round, sanguine face, lit up by two large, lively eyes." (p. 31). A conscientious employee, he owes his development to his marriage to Séverine: through her privileged relationship with President Grandmorin, he becomes deputy chief of the Havre station. But he is also a brutal and violent man who only obeys his instincts – he is frequently compared to an animal. When he learns of his wife's affair with Grandmorin, his jealousy drives him so mad that he brutally slits the president's throat on the train. After this murder, his life slowly deteriorates: he starts gambling, gets into debt, no longer communicates with his wife, and does not even react when he catches her in her lover's arms. He also seems more and more alienated from himself, wandering continuously between the station and the café. He is finally arrested for ordering the murder of Grandmorin and Séverine.

FLORE

Flore is the cousin of Jacques Lantier. She is "a tall girl of eighteen, blonde, strong, with a thick mouth, large greenish eyes, a low forehead, under heavy hair. She was not pretty, she had strong hips and the hard arms of a boy" (Chapter II). She is presented as a savage, in the image of the Croix-de-Maufras region, which she knows well, and is described as a strong woman of remarkable height. Her sister Louisette died after being abused by Grandmorin. She lives with her mother Phasie and her stepfather Misard in the gatehouse next to the Croix-de-Maufras.

She has been in love with Jacques for a long time, but repels all his suitors. Very jealous, she feels betrayed by her cousin when he takes Séverine as his mistress and feels the "savage instinct to destroy" (Chapter X). To kill the lovers, she causes a great railway disaster by pushing Cabuche's cart full of stones onto the tracks. Although the accident kills several people and injures many others, Lantier and Séverine escape unharmed. Unable to bear the horror of her action, she throws herself in front of a train: "Straightened up in her tall, supple statue-like stature, balanced on her strong legs, she moved forward. [...] And, in the dreadful shock, in the embrace, she straightened up again, as if, lifted up by a last revolt of a wrestler, she wanted to embrace the colossus, and strike him down." (*ibid.*)

KEYS TO READING

THE NATURALIST NOVEL

The history of the naturalist novel began in 1865 with the publication of *Germinie Lacerteux* by Edmond (1822-1896) and Jules (1830-1870) de Goncourt, which details the downfall of a country girl who arrives in Paris. The so-called naturalist writers were inspired by scientific methods of observation, especially thermodynamics and medicine. They thus took the work of the realists, who were mainly interested in the working classes, a step further and sought to evoke neuroses, madness, impulses and, in the context of *La Bête humaine*, what Zola called the "deaf vegetations of crime".

Zola's naturalism can be divided into two distinct periods. The first begins with the publication of *Mes Haines* (1866) and ends in 1878 with the reading of Claude Bernard's (physician-physiologist, 1813-1878) *Introduction à l'étude de la médecine expérimentale*. At this time he rejected the ideas of Hippolyte Taine (French philosopher, 1828-1893), who, in his view, gave far too much importance to determinism (the negation of free will) and did not take sufficient account of the question of personality. The second period of Zolian naturalism was the one during which he developed his doctrine of the experimental method, i.e. that the observation of a situation allows the formulation of hypotheses that experience will confirm or refute. In 1880 he published *Le roman expérimental,* a collection of articles in which he presented his new theory:

> *"The aim of the experimental method, in physiology and medicine, is to study phenomena in order to master them [...] this dream of the physiologist and the experimental doctor is also that of the novelist who applies the experimental method to the natural and social study of man [...]. [In a word, we are experimental moralists, showing by experiment how a passion behaves in a social environment.*

This experiment will be conducted through a family saga, *Les Rougon-Macquart.*

NATURALISM AND HEREDITY

"I want to explain how a family, a small group of beings, behaves in a society, by blossoming to give birth to ten, twenty individuals who appear, at first glance, profoundly dissimilar, but whom analysis shows to be intimately linked to each other. Heredity has its laws, like gravity," explains Zola in the preface to *La Fortune des Rougon,* the first volume of the novelistic saga of the Rougon-Macquarts. Starting from a double postulate – man is conditioned by his environment and by heredity – Zola placed his characters in a precise environment, then studied them in the manner of a doctor, describing the facts that were bound to occur in view of the basic postulates.

In *La Bête humaine,* Zola repeatedly emphasises the heavy family heritage that Jacques carries. He is the son of Gervaise Macquart, who died homeless in Paris after falling into alcoholism, and of Auguste Lantier, her lover, a man without morals. His great-grandmother,

Adélaïde Fouque, one of the main characters in *La Fortune des Rougon*, died insane, in an asylum. Several times in *La Bête humaine* it is mentioned that Jacques suffered strange attacks in his adolescence: pains would twist his skull, leave him feverish and depressed, or make him hide like an animal in a hole. These did not disappear with adulthood, but they were transformed into murderous impulses. For Zola, this defect is a burden bequeathed by his family: a crazy great-grandmother and an alcoholic mother could only produce a person who also suffers from psychological problems. Torn, Jacques struggles to keep these murderous desires away from him. He succeeds for a while and even thinks he has found happiness with Séverine. But his first instincts catch up with him and, at the end of the novel, he no longer controls himself and kills the young woman. Zola concludes with these words: "[...] He had just been swept away by the heredity of violence." (p. 419).

JACQUES AND THE LISON

Jacques, forced to flee from women, directed his love towards his locomotive, which is equated in the novel with a woman: "And it's true that he loved it with love, his machine, for the four years he had been driving it [...] If he loved that one, it was really because it had good qualities. [...] If he loved her, it was really because she had the qualities of a good woman." (p. 196). She is also named (the Lison) and even personified: "She was one of those express machines, with two coupled axles, of a fine and giant elegance, with her large light wheels joined by steel arms, her broad chest, her elongated and powerful loins." (p. 195). The lexical field used is one that would be used more to describe a human being: the machine is endowed with arms, with kidneys. Moreover, James looks after it and cares for it as one would a person.

After its meeting with Séverine, the Lison, which until then had been flawless, begins to function less well, as we discover in particular during the episode of the journey in the snow, when the train is blocked at the Croix-de-Maufras for a long time. When the engine starts up again, Jacques wonders whether his Lison was suffering from "serious internal disorders [...] nothing is more delicate than the complicated mechanism of the drawers, where the heart beats, the living soul" (p. 274). The locomotive thus gives the impression of reacting as if it were hurt by the relationship between its mechanic and Séverine.

A more general comparison between man and machine can be seen in the novel. Indeed, on several occasions, the frantic rhythm of the locomotive is compared, or at least paralleled, with the rhythm of human life, or even with the uncontrollable violence that characterises several characters in the novel. For example, the author describes the Le Havre express which "went off in its stormy violence, as if it had swept everything before it":

> *"It was a thunderbolt apparition: at once, the carriages followed one another, the small square windows of the doors, violently illuminated, paraded compartments full of travellers, in such a vertigo of speed, that the eye then doubted the images seen." (p. 90)*

This is a description of a machine that is launched at full speed, which nothing seems to be able to stop. This image is reminiscent of Roubaud's frenzied rise to violence in Chapter I, when he goes into a rage on learning of Séverine's affair with Grandmorin:

> *"Roubaud's fury never subsided. As soon as it seemed to dissipate a little, it returned at once, like drunkenness, in great redoubled waves, which carried him away in their dizziness. He no longer possessed himself, beat the void, thrown to all the jolts of the wind of violence with which he was flogged, falling back to the sole need to appease the howling beast within him. (p. 53)*

Man, like the machine, cannot be stopped when caught by such destructive impulses.

A CRIME NOVEL

The press of the time was very keen on criminal cases and one often finds in its pages a summary of certain trials. Zola himself wrote an account of the trial of the three Marseilles poisoners for *La Tribune*, a famous case of the time. Faced with this craze, the writer wanted to include a "legal novel" in the *Rougon-Macquart* cycle: this was, of course, *La Bête humaine*. At the time, Zola was living in Médan, on the edge of the railway line linking Paris to Le Havre. He therefore imagined the setting for his work by seeing the train pass before his eyes every day.

The Human Beast is a novel full of violence that tells the story of several crimes, the first of which, that of Grandmorin, leads to all the others. People kill very easily, and always for vile reasons such as jealousy, greed, or a taste for blood. In the face of such brutality, killing becomes, as the plot progresses, an increasingly banal act. At the beginning, when Roubaud decides to murder Grandmorin, he sets up a clever and cold-blooded trap. Later, wishing to get rid of her husband to live with her lover, Séverine asks Jacques to kill Roubaud, quite simply, without obviously feeling any remorse or being torn by her conscience. In fact, at no time does Roubaud feel the slightest fear about his act. He has killed Grandmorin, but does not regret it, even if it causes him great excitement and intense nervousness. Jacques also desires to kill. It is even part of his being, since he has felt murderous impulses since he was very young: "Oh! to give such a stab, to satisfy this distant desire, to know what one feels, to taste this minute when one lives more than in one's entire existence." (p. 299). Only, when Séverine asks him to kill her husband, Jacques is unable to do so. For him, the crime must come from an impulse, not from reflection, it must be the result of a sudden urge. For this reason, he will let Roubaud live but will kill Séverine.

The study of Jacques' character is a fundamental part of the work. Like Dostoyevsky (Russian novelist, 1821-1881) in *Crime and Punishment* (1866) – a novel in which the soul of the hero, a criminal, is studied at length, dissected, in order to understand the reasons that drove him to the crime and the feelings that inhabit him once his deed has been done – Zola discusses Lantier's personality at length. He is a man who has always been inhabited by evil, since his murderous impulses manifested themselves very early in his life. He is the victim of a sort of split personality, a duality like Dr Jekyll and Mr Hyde in the eponymous novel by Stevenson (Scottish writer, 1850-1894): Jacques feels these impulses, but he tries at all costs to avoid murder. In this respect, it can be said that Zola is truly describing a "human beast", an animal with a human face that will eventually be caught up in its bestiality.

AVENUES FOR REFLECTION

SOME IDEAS FOR FURTHER REFLECTION...

- Explain the title of the work in relation to your reading.

- How does Cabuche differ from the other characters in the novel?

- Study the evolution of Severine's character. Would you place her on the side of the victims or on the side of the perpetrators? Justify your answer.

- To what extent is Jacques Lantier the master of his destiny?

- What image of love does Zola present in his novel?

- In *La Bête humaine*, there is a lot of talk about justice. How does Zola treat this concept? What vision does he give of it?

- What historical indications are given in the novel? Can we say that *La Bête humaine* is a historical novel? Explain.

- In what way can this novel be said to be naturalistic? Please elaborate.

- What role does the village of La Croix de Maufras play in the plot? Why does Jacques have a strange feeling every time he goes there? Develop your answer using concrete examples.

- In your opinion, is the railway environment a simple setting for the story? Justify your answer.

TO GO FURTHER

REFERENCE EDITION

Zola É., *La Bête humaine*, Paris, Gallimard, « Folio classique » collection, 2003, 512 p.

BENCHMARK STUDIES

Becker C., *Le roman naturaliste*, Paris, Bréal, coll. « Connaissance d'un thème », 1999.

Becker C., *Lire le réalisme et le naturalisme*, Paris, Armand Colin, coll. « Lettres sup. », 2010.

Mitterand H., *Zola et le naturalisme*, Paris, PUF, « Que sais-je ?

Noël L., « Le principe du déterminisme », in *Revue néo-scolastique*, n° 45, 1905.

ADAPTATIONS

La Bête humaine, film by Jean Renoir, screenplay by Jean Renoir, with Jean Gabin, Simone Signoret and Fernand Ledoux, France, 1938.

Human Desires, film by Fritz Lang, screenplay by Alfred Hayes, with Glenn Ford and Gloria Grahame, USA, 1954.

Your opinion is important to us!
Leave a comment on the website of your online bookshop
and share your favourites on social networks!

Ebook EAN: 9782808686594
Paperback EAN: 9782808697996
Legal Deposit: D/2023/12603/1079

Cover: © Primento
Digital conception by Primento, the digital partner of publishers.